Book Club Weekly Reader Children's Book Cl
's Book Club Weekly Reader Children's Book Cl
n's Book Club Weekly Reader Children's Book
en's Book Club Weekly Reader Children's Book
dren's Book Club Weekly Reader Children's Bo
ldren's Book Club Weekly Reader Children's Bo
hildren's Book Club Weekly Reader Children's B
Children's Book Club Weekly Reader Children's
Children's Book Club Weekly Reader Children'
er Children's Book Club Weekly Reader Childre
der Children's Book Club Weekly Reader Childr
ader Children's Book Club Weekly Reader Child
eader Children's Book Club Weekly Reader Chi
Reader Children's Book Club Weekly Reader C
y Reader Children's Book Club Weekly Reader
ly Reader Children's Book Club Weekly Reade
ekly Reader Children's Book Club Weekly Read
eekly Reader Children's Book Club Weekly Rea
Weekly Reader Children's Book Club Weekly Re
b Weekly Reader Children's Book Club Weekly R
ub Weekly Reader Children's Book Club Weekly
lub Weekly Reader Children's Book Club Weekl
Club Weekly Reader Children's Book Club Wee
Club Weekly Reader Children's Book Club We
k Club Weekly Reader Children's Book Club W
ekly Reader Children's Book Club

For Rosemary Courtney!
Best wishes from [illegible]

Weekly Reader Children's Book Club presents

Maude and Claude Go Abroad

By Susan Meddaugh

Houghton Mifflin Company · Boston

This book is a presentation of
Weekly Reader Children's Book Club.

Weekly Reader Children's Book Club
offers book clubs for children from
preschool through junior high school.
All quality hardcover books are selected by
a distinguished Weekly Reader Selection Board.

For further information write to:
Weekly Reader Children's Book Club
1250 Fairwood Ave.
Columbus, Ohio 43216

Library of Congress Cataloging in Publication Data

Meddaugh, Susan.
Maude and Claude go abroad.

SUMMARY: While cruising to France, a sister and brother go overboard and encounter a whale who is being pursued by harpooners.
[1. Brothers and sisters – Fiction. 2. Whales – Fiction. 3. Stories in rhyme] I. Title.
PZ8.3.M55115Mau [E] 79-26460
ISBN 0-395-29162-3

Printed in the United States of America.

For John and Debi

Father and Mother
sent Maude and her brother
to visit their favorite aunts.
These two — on their own —
sailed off from their home,
for faraway Phox-en-ville, France.

SS REYNARD

"Take care of your brother.
You haven't another,"
said Mother to Maude who was older.
"Please keep him in sight
all day and all night."
"I promise I will," Maudie told her.

The porter took Maude
and her brother Claude
to a room that was theirs for the trip.
"This stateroom's a great room,"
said Claude. "I can't wait
to explore every floor of this ship."

CREW ONLY
GALLEY
OUT

S S REYNARD
№6

Claude had to inspect
every spot on the deck.
No nautical nook was neglected.
Sighed Maude, "This is hard.
The S.S. *Reynard*
is far bigger than I expected."

Unfortunately,
on the third day at sea,
Claude ran off alone to the stern.
And as they were sailing,
he climbed up the railing
and balanced there feeding a tern.

Maude knew in a flash,
when she heard a big splash,
that her brother had gone in the water.
What else could she do
but jump over too?
For Maude was a dutiful daughter.

S.S. REYNARD

S.S. REYNARD

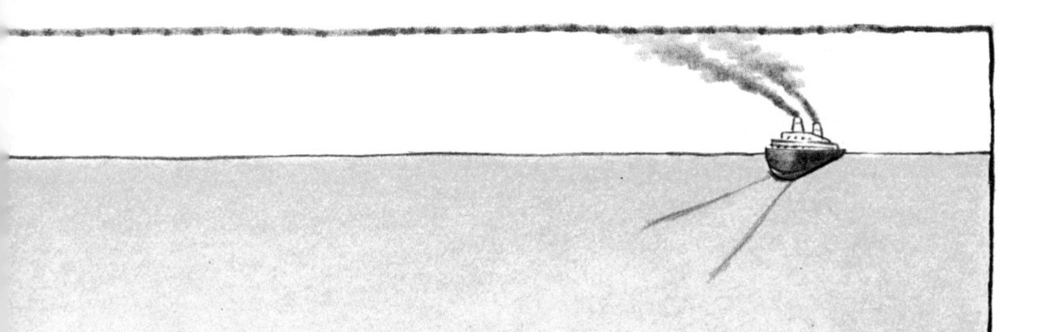

Claude giggled, "What fun."

But Maude was undone.

She looked up and said with dismay,

"I'm glad you can float,

because there goes the boat."

And they watched as it sailed far away.

Then up from the deep
rose a mountain so steep,
a creature of towering size.
He looked out of breath
and half scared to death.
"A whale!" Maudie said with surprise.

She cried, "We are saved!"
She shouted and waved.
The whale only gasped as he passed her:
"I'd stop if I could,
but I can't, for it would
surely lead to an awful disaster."

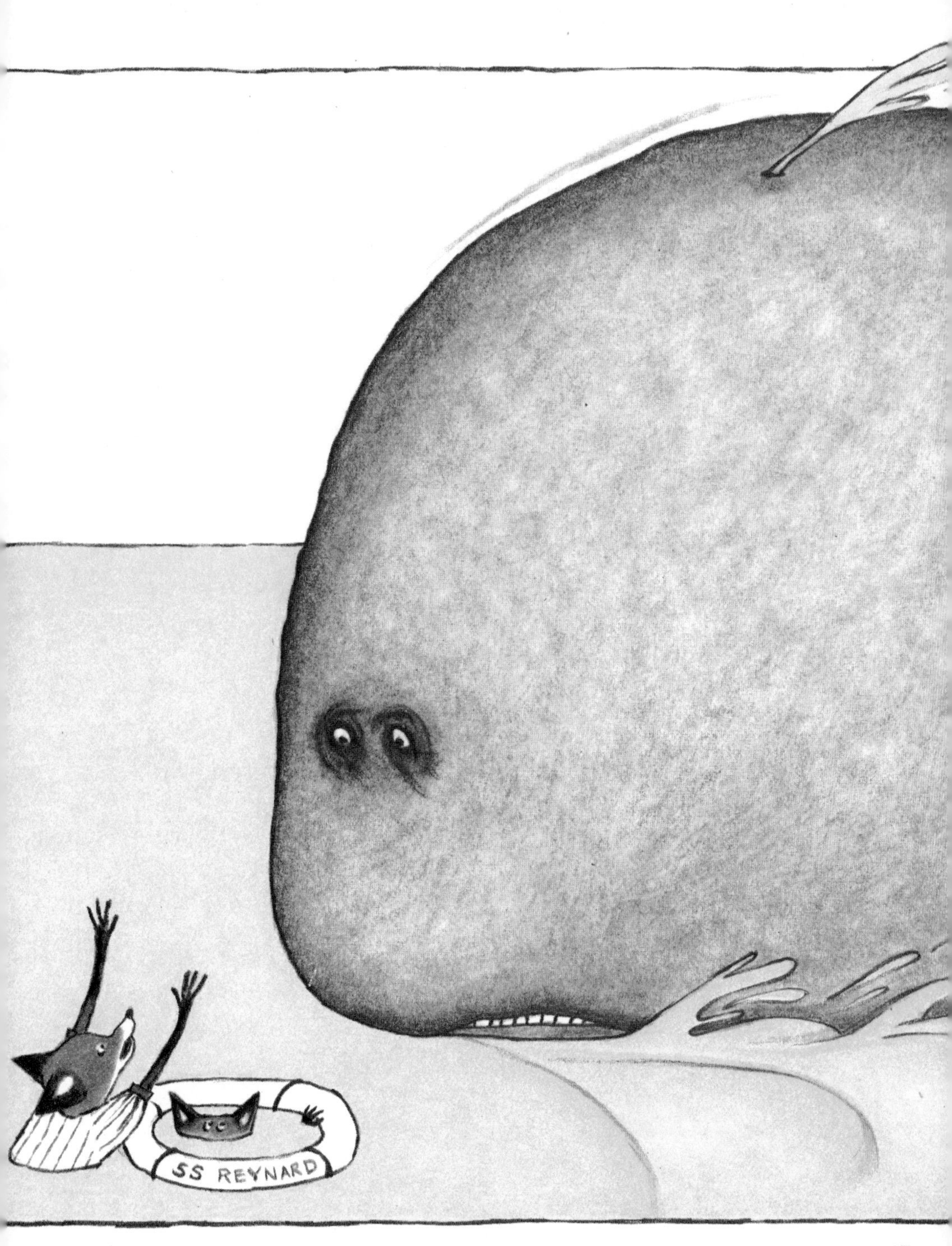
SS REYNARD

"A ship under sail
is hot on my trail.
The crew on this ship has one notion.
They don't think of me
as king of the sea
but as valuable blubber in motion.

"I'm beat and I'm busted.
My insides are rusted.
I'm tired and I've had a spoutful!"
"We'll help you to hide,
if you'll give us a ride,"
Maudie cried to the whale, who looked doubtful.

"We'll sit on your spout
so no water comes out.
We'll look like we're sitting on dry land.
Submerging your tail,
you won't look like a whale.
You'll really look more like an island."

The big fellow gazed
out over the waves.
His spout spurted short nervous squirts.
Then he said, "I'm willing."
And Claude said, "How thrilling!"
And Maude said, "I do hope this works."

Maude heard the whale gulp
as the whale ship sailed up.
She felt a small tremble run through him.
A cruel-looking creature
with menacing features
leaned over the side and said to them:

"Avast there, landlubbers!
We're fast after blubber.
Have you seen a gray whale today?
We were right behind him,
but now we can't find him."
And Maude said, "He went thataway!"

BAD DOG

Then Maude heard him hiss,
"What island is this?
I do not recall it at all.

I'll look it up later
for we cannot wait or
our profits will be much too small.

"So, full speed ahead!"
the mean captain said
to his scurvy old crew on the schooner.
The whale with delight
watched the ship sail from sight,
and with it each nasty harpooner.

"How can I repay you?"
he asked. "Did you say you
were rideless?" And Maudie replied,
"We're due at our aunts'
in Phox-en-ville, France,
and we certainly could use a ride."

They sailed to the east
on their stately old beast,
sunny days, starry nights in slow motion.
And as they were cruising
the whale told amusing
and colorful tales of the ocean.

At last came the day
Maudie heard the whale say,
"That's France in the distance, you know."
As Maudie laid eyes on
land on the horizon,
he said, "That's as far as I go."

"I'll miss you both awfully,"
their whale friend said softly.
"Please think of me now and again."
And Maudie said sadly,
"I promise you that we
will think of you often, my friend."

PHOX-EN-VILLE
OVER THE HILL

Maude later declared,
"What adventure we've shared,
all because of my promise to Mother.
It just goes to show
how caring can grow,
even when it starts out with your brother!"

der Chil
ader Children's Bo
eader Children's Book Club Wee
Reader Children's Book Club Weekly Reade
y Reader Children's Book Club Weekly Reader Chil
ly Reader Children's Book Club Weekly Reader Chi
ekly Reader Children's Book Club Weekly Reader C
eekly Reader Children's Book Club Weekly Reader
Weekly Reader Children's Book Club Weekly Reade
Weekly Reader Children's Book Club Weekly Reac
b Weekly Reader Children's Book Club Weekly Re
ub Weekly Reader Children's Book Club Weekly R
Club Weekly Reader Children's Book Club Weekly
Club Weekly Reader Children's Book Club Weekl
k Club Weekly Reader Children's Book Club Week
ok Club Weekly Reader Children's Book Club We
Book Club Weekly Reader Children's Book Club W
s Book Club Weekly Reader Children's Book Club
n's Book Club Weekly Reader Children's Book Clu
en's Book Club Weekly Reader Children's Book C
dren's Book Club Weekly Reader Children's Book
ildren's Book Club Weekly Reader Children's Boo
hildren's Book Club Weekly Reader Children's Bo
Children's Book Club Weekly Reader Children's B
Children's Book Club Weekly Reader Children's
dren's Book Club Weekly Reader Children